		EssexWorks.
		For a better quality of life
2 3 APR 2012		ING
9 JUN 2012		
	− 6 MAR 2017	
	1 6 AUG 2017	
	1 4 NOV 2019	

Please return this book on or before the date shown above. To renew go to www.essex.gov.uk/libraries, ring 0845 603 7628 or go to any Essex library.

Essex County Council

For Lewis
R.I.

For Emilio
R.A.

ORCHARD BOOKS
338 Euston Road, London NW1 3BH
Orchard Books Australia
Hachette Children's Books
Level 17/207 Kent Street, Sydney, NSW 2000

First published in Great Britain in 2006
First paperback publication 2007

Text © Rose Impey 2006
Illustrations © Russell Ayto 2006

A CIP catalogue record for this book is available from the British Library

ISBN 978 1 84362 231 4

3 5 7 9 10 8 6 4 2

Printed in China

Orchard Books is a division of Hachette Children's Books,
an Hachette Livre UK company.
www.hachettechildrens.co.uk

MONSTER AND Frog
GET FIT

ROSE IMPEY 🦴 RUSSELL AYTO

ORCHARD BOOKS

Frog wants to get fit. He tells Monster he should get fit too.

But Monster is happy as he is.

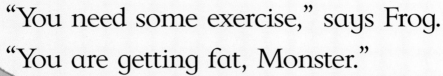

"You need some exercise," says Frog.
"You are getting fat, Monster."

Monster looks down at his tummy.

"Leave it to me," says Frog.
"I know all about exercise."

"First," says Frog, "we will try jogging."
Monster has never been jogging before.

Jogging?

But Frog is an expert at jogging.
Monster and Frog jog down
the road. Monster starts to huff
and puff.

"I feel better already," says Frog.

But Monster does not feel better.

Sweat runs into his eyes.

He cannot see where he is going.

Monster is covered with cuts
and bruises.

He tells Frog, "Monsters do
not jog."

Frog says, "We will try
swimming next."
Monster has never been
swimming before.

"I will show you," says Frog.
"Swimming is what frogs do best."

Monster and Frog go to the
swimming pool.
The water looks deep.
Frog dives in. "Follow me," he calls.

But Monster does not know
about diving.
He does a belly flop instead.

CRASH!
SPLASH!

Monster sinks to the bottom
of the pool.
When he comes up, his eyes
and nose are full of water.

"Monsters do *not* swim either!"
he tells Frog.

"Do not worry," says Frog. "We
will soon find the right exercise
for monsters."

Frog takes Monster to a gym.
Monster has never been to
a gym before.

Frog shows Monster how to
hop and jump. Frog is an expert
at hopping and jumping.
But Monster cannot get off
the ground.

Next they try skipping.
"Skipping is very easy," says Frog.
"Watch me."

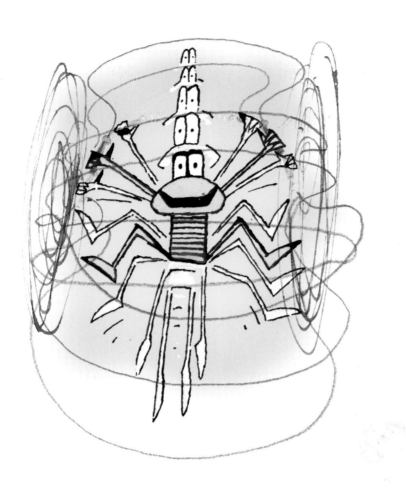

Frog skips so fast he is just a blur.
Frog makes skipping look easy.

But when Monster tries to skip,
his tail gets in the way.

The rope wraps itself around
his ankles.
Monster falls to the ground like
a tree.

BOOM!

Monster throws the rope on
the floor.

"Monsters do *not* jog," he says,
"they do *not* swim and they
definitely do *not* skip!"

But Frog will not give up.
"Weightlifting is good exercise,"
he says. "It is my speciality."

But when Frog tries to lift the weights, he heaves and grunts and turns a funny colour.

"Hmmm," he croaks. "Weights are not as easy as they look."

But then Monster tries.
He lifts one weight
in each hand.

He lifts them high above
his head.

Monster throws the weights in
the air and catches them.

Weights are easy for monsters.
Monsters *do* like weightlifting.
Now Monster is starting to feel fit.

"Coming to the gym was your best idea yet," Monster tells Frog. "I bet you are glad you thought of it!"

ROSE IMPEY ❧ RUSSELL AYTO

Enjoy all these adventures with Monster and Frog!

Monster and Frog and the Big Adventure
978 1 84362 228 4
Monster and Frog Get Fit
978 1 84362 231 4
Monster and Frog and the Slippery Wallpaper
978 1 84362 230 7
Monster and Frog Mind the Baby
978 1 84362 232 1
Monster and Frog and the Terrible Toothache
978 1 84362 227 7
Monster and Frog and the All-in-Together Cake
978 1 84362 233 8
Monster and Frog and the Haunted Tent
978 1 84362 229 1
Monster and Frog and the Magic Show
978 1 84362 234 5

All priced at £4.99

Orchard Colour Crunchies are available from all good bookshops, or can be ordered
direct from the publisher: Orchard Books, PO BOX 29, Douglas IM99 1BQ
Credit card orders please telephone 01624 836000
or fax 01624 837033 or visit our Internet site: www.wattspub.co.uk
or e-mail: bookshop@enterprise.net for details.

To order please quote title, author and ISBN
and your full name and address.
Cheques and postal orders should be made payable to 'Bookpost plc.'
Postage and packing is FREE within the UK
(overseas customers should add £1.00 per book).

Prices and availability are subject to change.